La Blanche

La Blanche

Maï-Do Hamisultane

Translated from the French by
Suzy Ceulan Hughes

PARTHIAN

Co-funded by the Creative Europe Programme of the European Union

This book is supported by the Institut français (Royaume-Uni) as part of the Burgess programme

Maï-Do Hamisultane is a Franco-Moroccan writer born in La Rochelle in 1983. After a childhood spent between Cap d'Antibes and Casablanca, she studied at the Lycée Janson-de-Sailly in Paris, before going on to study medicine and specialise in psychiatry. As the literary critic Meriem El Youssoufi points out, the literary works of Maï-Do Hamisultane navigate between the real and the imaginary. *La Blanche* was nominated for the prestigious Prix La Mamounia in 2014. Hamisultane's other work includes *Santo Sospir* (2015), and *Lettres à Abel* (2017).

Suzy Ceulan Hughes is a writer and translator. Her own short stories have been included in anthologies, and her translations of short fiction by Marie Darrieussecq and Scholastique Mukasonga have been published in *New Welsh Review/Reader* (Issues 102 and 111). In 2015, she was awarded joint third prize in the John Dryden Translation Competition for her translation from *Kant et la petite robe rouge* by Lamia Berrada-Berca (published in *Comparative Critical Studies*, Volume 13, Number 1, 2016).

Parthian, Cardigan SA43 1ED
www.parthianbooks.com
First published in French in 2013

ISBN 978-1-912681-23-5
Editor: Carly Holmes
Cover design: Syncopated Pandemonium
Cover image: Glen Pearson/Millennium Images, UK
Typeset by Elaine Sharples
Printed in EU by Pulsio SARL
Published with the financial support of the Welsh Books Council and Institut français (Royaume-Uni) as part of the Burgess programme
Co-funded by the Creative Europe Programme of the European Union
British Library Cataloguing in Publication Data
A cataloguing record for this book is available from the British Library.

Introduction

I first read *La Blanche*, Maï-Do Hamisultane's debut novella, soon after it was published in French in 2013. I was immediately struck by its intensity and concision, by how much it embraced in so few pages. Several years and numerous readings later, I realise there is always something more to discover in a narrative that works on so many levels – from a compelling murder mystery, to a deep contemplation of our human complexity and our unknowability, to ourselves and to each other.

When she was nine, Hamisultane's Moroccan grandfather was murdered in his own home. This is the story that lies at the core of the novella, an intricate weaving of fact and fiction about a tragic death and its consequences, both immediate and long-term, on the lives and perceptions of everyone touched by it. Hamisultane is an enigmatic storyteller, and the fact that *La Blanche* is fictionalised autobiography adds a further layer of intrigue. On a purely superficial level, there is room for common curiosity: did the family home really have gardens large enough to accommodate *les fantasias*, traditional north African displays of horsemanship? Was there really a black briefcase with a gold combination lock, and if so, what was in it? In this, the book could be seen as almost playful, making the most of our passion for a good story and our addiction to solving puzzles. But this interweaving of the real and the imaginary is also the surface reflection of a deeper question that we seem driven to explore, and which is very much to the forefront in a world of fake news. What is real? What is true? Where is the divide between fact and fiction?

Something I didn't initially recognise in *La Blanche* is the way in which Hamisultane quietly embeds references and allusions to the work of other writers. This, of course, is another game that some readers like to play: spot the literary allusion. English-speaking readers are at a disadvantage here though, and we have perhaps spoiled the fun by flagging them, giving the title of the work and the author's name, for readers to follow through if they wish. We have flagged only the references confirmed by Hamisultane, but I still wonder whether there might be more. I thought I had spotted one to the great Moroccan writer, Tahar Ben Jelloun, but Hamisultane said no, and slightly changed the French for me. I also asked her to let me know if there were others that I had failed to recognise. She didn't confirm either way. So perhaps there are still hidden gems for readers to discover.

La Blanche is the work of a young writer of fierce intelligence and considerable courage. Hamisultane is not afraid to experiment with narrative style and structure. She freely draws on painful personal experiences. And she is brave enough to leave the reader with unanswered questions to ponder.

Suzy Ceulan Hughes 2019

For more information on the translation process and on the influence of Marguerite Duras, please see 'Mastering Marguerite', in *New Welsh Reader*, Issue 119.

‘I saw the clown’s clothes and the blue kohl around your eyes. Then I knew I was right, and that I loved you because, contrary to all I’d been taught, you were neither a layabout nor a murderer; you had just opted out of life.’

Marguerite Duras, *Blue Eyes, Black Hair*

'There is a small key. All you have to do is turn it.'

Luc

Return

Franklin Roosevelt. The boulevard that runs down to the Atlantic Ocean. Casablanca. Twenty years ago, I think. The taxi speeds along. The driver is taking me from the airport to a hotel by the sea. He talks a lot. He talks to me as if I were a foreigner. I prefer it that way. I answer him, though my mind is elsewhere, as though I'm trying not to see or hear or smell the past that is hitting me in the face through the wide-open window. We go around one of the few bends in the road and the worn tarmac turns into memories. The same thirsty trees with their white trunks. The governor's house, which hasn't changed. I know we're going to drive past Mira Ventos. So I close my eyes, which are full of tears. It's already too much for me. I'm scared of realising that the only thing that belongs to us is what we have lost.
Tomorrow, I'll come back.
Yes, I'll face it all tomorrow.

Twenty years, forty perhaps… Why count how many years have passed, when every one of them is so agonising? I got up very early this morning, because that's when you can really smell the fresh, iodine tang of the Atlantic. The huge expanse of waterlogged sand stretches to the horizon. Walking for hours on wet sand. Allowing your bare feet to sink into it. Walking. Leaving your footprints on the surface. Being followed. Not being followed. Wandering aimlessly. Losing yourself. Losing yourself there and leaving your footprints to drown in the foaming froth of the Atlantic. A crazy wish to melt into the

smells of childhood. I'm alone on the beach. There's just a throbbing groan, as though someone is blowing into a huge seashell.
I suddenly feel that I'm no longer alone. Perhaps because the tide is starting to come in, making the beach smaller. I look behind me. I see a figure appear, on the shore, in the distance. A shiver runs through me. I feel terribly cold.

Childhood is innocence, even if it sometimes comes to an end at an early age. I don't remember when I lost mine, but they say the memory of it comes back when you reconnect with the cause of its loss.

I've called a taxi to take me to Mira Ventos. My white house with the strangely green roof tiles seems to have died. I shudder as I enter my home, a trespasser.
The grass that used to be green and fresh is scorched and threadbare. The huge, zellige-tiled fountain is dry, in the midst of a dead garden whose glory days are gone. I sit on the ground. Then I lie down, as though I too am dying of neglect. I think I must have fallen asleep.

Years Earlier

Mira Ventos is resplendent.
It is midday.
Fatima is carrying silver dishes to the table laid out formally on the lawn. The whole family is here. The laughter that fills the air is mingled with the sound of water. It is terribly hot.
My cousins are running around all over the place. And, with my child's eyes, I watch a whole world that is about to fall apart. It never occurred to me that I was going to miss them. I was living in the moment.

It took just a month to sell the house, which is emptied little by little. Almost every member of the family wanted to take something away with them. And how big a Moroccan family is at such times! The vast, white marble living room, the height of sophistication, echoed with solitude. This living space had become our refuge.
At midday, in the garden, we had managed to forget, for the space of a lunchtime. We'd managed to forget the irrevocable that makes solitude unbearable. I was nine years old, I think, and I wasn't thinking about the consequences. I waited impatiently for them all to go home so the place would be mine again. Then I pulled off the great white sheets that were draped over the huge mirrors in the dining room, and at last I could watch myself dancing to the tinny sound of the record turning and turning. I didn't understand why the mirrors had to be covered for forty days, but I loved wearing the fine, white cotton djellabas.

Yesterday, the house was sold to a fat, ugly German. I find it hard to accept that this swaggering pig is taking possession of my world. From a distance, I see my grandmother smile, something I don't see her do very often now. I'm happy, even though my child's intuition tells me she's being swindled by the honey-tongued swine, who's shaking the hennaed hands of the women who are weeping for someone they never really knew.

My grandmother comes hurrying towards me and, taking me by surprise, lifts me up into the air in a gesture of victory – I'm going to get you out of here, dear child!

She tells me triumphantly that we're going back to France.

She tells me about the peace and quiet, about the cockerel crowing and our family over there.

Tomorrow, we're going on a tour around the country before the grand departure. Théophile Gautier. The French mission. We've thrown helium-filled balloons into the air.

Everyone has put a message inside a balloon.

Alexandre knows I'm leaving. Who'll be his scapegoat now?

He comes up to me. His big blue eyes search my face.

'What was your message?' he asks me.

'It's none of your business.'

'My message is for you.'

'What is it?'

'Trust in fate. If you're meant to know what it is, then this balloon will end up finding you.'

It wasn't the answer I was expecting any more.

I think I smiled.

Grandma and I drove across Morocco in her improbably violet Peugeot. A bit like Thelma and Louise, I caught myself thinking.

With the headlines still constantly referring to the tragedy that was

hitting us too closely, my imposing yet gracious grandmother hid behind a large pair of sunglasses and an enormous straw hat, which only served to draw attention to us.
It's strange. I knew we were running away. Our escapade felt illicit. I didn't feel like a victim any more; I felt guilty. But guilty of what? I wouldn't know until much later.

Tangier. The fresh sea air of the Atlantic. White lime-washed houses. Royal-blue zellige tiles hidden away in internal courtyards with white marble fountains.
Le Mirage Hotel. A colonial world where various artists, feigning anonymity, stayed in chalets around the swimming pool overlooking the Atlantic.
A dark-haired young man followed me when I was going down the long, white stairway to the sea. He caught up with me and we swam naked in the Atlantic. Although I was so young, I was strongly attracted by his smooth, dark skin.
In the evening, the hotel manager told us that members of the Yale university choir were staying there. I was embarrassed to see among the young Americans the face of the body that had made rings in the water with mine that morning.

I don't know how many days our brief escapade lasted, but it seems like forever now. We picked Mum up on the way back. We'd left her at a nursing home near Casablanca after she had her breakdown; she needed treatment.

We have to sleep at Mira Ventos tonight. It's the last night before we leave.

The Clown of Casablanca

I'm so scared at Mira Ventos at night. All night we keep checking that all the doors and windows are closed and locked. We don't trust anyone any more. The servants were sent home in the evening. It's just us; three women alone in this land of men. Mum, my grandmother and I sleep together in the big bed in the nursery. The nursery door is also locked. We've pushed the chest of drawers up against the door as well, just in case. I even have a sharp knife under my pillow. I haven't told anyone. It's my secret weapon. And who'd begrudge me that? Mum can't say anything: she has a revolver. She knows that I know. She made me promise not to tell my grandmother. But she lied to me: she told me it wasn't loaded.

It's morning at Mira Ventos. I'm lying in the garden. I don't go out for walks around the neighbourhood any more. I know I wouldn't be allowed. It's too dangerous. And anyway, I don't feel like it. It would make me think of my grandfather, still alive, and then of his death and his murder. I can't cope with those shifting feelings, from joy to regret and anger.

I want to feel light-hearted, without a care in the world, to escape this sadness washing over me, that I have no wish to bear.

Mira Ventos. Its whiteness.

Its big trees laden with fruit.

Mira Ventos breathes.

You wouldn't think there had just been a murder here. They say people

are marked by sad events in their lives only long after they've happened, sometimes even after they've been forgotten. It's as though life is determined to reduce people to their past, denying them the freedom to start again. Is that what will happen to Mira Ventos?
Its zellige-tiled fountain softly singing. The sound of water. The green. The shades of green. White. The hundred-year-old trees with all their colour tones. The huge palm trees of another century. The hibiscus hedge constantly in flower. The rose bushes breathing out their scent. The snapdragons that make us laugh when we pinch their mouths open. The lawn that is always green, even after the long, hot days of summer.
Mira Ventos, ever alive.
Immersing myself forever in its universe.
When he saw me looking at the pomegranates, grapefruits and mandarins, Hassan came over to me with a ladder.
The two of us set off to raid the fruit trees.
Then he took a pomegranate from our spoils. He cut it open for me with a Swiss army knife he'd taken out of the pocket of his fake Levi's. I hadn't seen a pomegranate before and, when he cut it open, it looked as though it was full of rubies.

Tonight, like every night, I wait for the sun to rise before really going to sleep. I'd like us to have watches, like on a ship, so there's always someone keeping guard. But Grandma would think I was mad. And, as she says, it's more her tragedy than mine.
The sky begins to lighten at last. It feels so good to end the watch in the embrace of the morning sun.

I don't go to school any more. In any case, I couldn't bear any more of their kindness. I wanted to tell them to fuck off. Just fuck off, all of you. And I like staying with my mother and grandmother. I like our enclosed life, just the three of us.

The barrister came for lunch today. He talked a lot, but he didn't say very much. He talked about the court case that was going to start without a defendant. My grandmother was the only one at home the night of the tragedy.
Fatima and Hassan had taken the night off.
Grandma has to go to the police station to identify suspects.

Mum wants me to go back to school. I don't want to. I spend my time reading, lying on the freshly mown lawn, close to the fountain.
There are all sorts of books in Grandma's mahogany library. *The Opposing Shore*, *The Parting of the Waters*, *Midnight Mass*, *The Ravishing of Lol Stein*, and *Song Offerings* by someone called Rabindranath Tagore. All sorts of books that appeal to my imagination and fill me with curiosity. I can see myself now, pronouncing the Indian author's name, Rabindranath Tagore, slowly, enthralled, trying to savour every syllable, each one making me shiver with delight, as though with each of them I was breathing in air laden with unfamiliar scents. I began to discover armchair travel.
Grandma came in and looked at me with a knowing smile. She stepped onto the bottom rung of the wooden library steps. They creaked. I was scared they might at any moment give way beneath her and that my grandmother would fall. At last she came down and handed me *The Sheltering Sky* by Paul Bowles, saying, 'You're a bit too young to understand, but I think you'll like it.'
And she disappeared as suddenly as she'd arrived.
I opened the book.
On the first page were the words:

> *'Each man's destiny is personal only insofar as it may resemble what is already in his memory.'*
>
> Eduardo Mallea

I didn't understand until much later.

Mum is cross with me for shutting myself away so much. For not wanting her to invite other children to play with me. But it's not what I want. I'm fine. I don't want anyone else coming to Mira Ventos. In any case, other people can only do us harm.
I imagine Alexandre's mocking laugh, the other children asking me questions, destroying the privacy of Mira Ventos.
Grandpa's murder has been front-page news ever since the night of the crime. They might have stopped mentioning it by now, but it's important to my grandmother. She phones the editor of one of the biggest daily newspapers every day, to make sure that people keep talking about the tragedy that has shattered our family, so the case doesn't get shelved and lost in the police archives, as happens with so many crimes in Morocco.

Mum took me fishing for periwinkles. On the rocks sticking up here and there on a huge, wet beach. It was misty. I recently came across a photo of the outing, which I'd always thought was preserved only in my memory.
My shadow fidgets about there. My hands wander in the sand. Then suddenly, nothing. A human shadow. Huge. Which instantly stops me in my tracks. I turn around. In the distance, I see a woman on the cliff. I'm scared. I run out of this shadow that's swallowing up my own.
Mum made me put the periwinkles back in the water. I wanted to break them, to see what they looked like inside their coiled shells. To see them naked. Completely naked.
People told me I was naughty, but it isn't true. I'm curious, that's all.
On the way home in the car, through the half-open window, I let my face hang a little longer in the sea spray of the Atlantic. I breathe very deeply. I open my eyes again. I see the woman we saw earlier moving off in the distance. She's like one of those wild dogs there are so many of on Moroccan beaches. A shiver runs through my body. I quickly point the woman out to Mum, as she disappears on the horizon.

Mum told me she was the clown of Casablanca. That she'd been wandering around Sidi Abderrahmane for years. Then she said she was tired out. That she'd tell me later.

My grandmother has been invited to supper by one of her author friends. They call each other 'sweetie'. So this evening Fatima hasn't prepared anything for supper because we'll be dining with sweetie, who isn't sweet at all.
As soon as we arrive, a black, bare-chested servant waddles up to us. Mum stares at the leopard-print fabric wrapped around his waist, which is all he's wearing. We walk through several reception rooms. The apartment is one of old-fashioned luxury that clashes with the squalid neighbourhood around it. We can hear bursts of laughter.
Eventually we come upon the scene of a dozen men wriggling about around a long, rectangular table of dark walnut littered with Bohemian crystal, red wine and dusty silverware. I can tell Mum is ill at ease. But my grandmother seems to know most of them. I switched my mind off for the entire meal. I didn't let myself touch a thing.

On our way home we did a detour via McDonald's, which had just opened on the beachfront.
Afterwards we passed the woman they call the clown of Casablanca. Before we went to sleep, Mum told me the woman's story. I couldn't stop thinking about the clown of Casablanca all night. Who would've thought that this woman, mocked by the lowest of the low, was once the envy of all?

My grandmother had told Mum the story. She was young and had just joined my grandfather in Morocco. They'd been invited to one of those sumptuous weddings thrown by local bigwigs. It was the wedding of one of the most sought-after young women. Her father adored her and had allowed her to marry 'for love' a man he didn't approve of. He had given in to the ultimate whim of his beloved daughter, which was to break away from him.

It was hot.

Very hot.

Thousands of guests from all parts of the country were dressed in muslin stitched with gold thread.

The women's cheering cries hovered in the air.

My grandmother had never seen such pomp and ceremony. The press was there.

The bride-to-be is soon to make her entrance in one of the Moroccan reception rooms. The one reserved for women.

People are getting impatient.

The atmosphere becomes heavy.

The women's cheering cries turn into hushed murmurings.

There's a terrible scream.

Then nothing.

Everything is cancelled.

Soon afterwards, people heard the young twenty-one-year-old had been jilted on her wedding day for another woman. She never got over it. She disappeared for a long time. A lot of people said she'd fled her misery by going abroad, more specifically to France. Others said she'd been sectioned.

Fatima, who had friends who worked at the house, brought the true story to Mira Ventos. The father was looking after his beloved child, who had lost her mind, at home, keeping her close to him. He died a few years later. His much-loved daughter, having ordered all the mirrors to be removed, made up her face by guesswork, doing everything she could to stifle her grief beneath random layers of make-up.

Burying her face beneath thick layers until she could no longer recognise herself. Leaving behind her childhood dreams and illusions.

She hurried away from the family home, where the body of her devoted father lay. And she walked for a long time before ending up on the shore of Sidi Abderrahmane.

Mum thinks the clown of Casablanca is magnificent in her grief. I think the woman's ridiculous. She sends a shiver down my spine. I've always hated clowns. They're anything but funny. They are terrifying. And I really don't understand how a woman can lose her dignity to such a point because of a man. There are so many men around.
Alexandre rang the doorbell today. But he says he doesn't love me. He came because the newspapers are full of the tragedy. He came to gawp. Through the window I watch him get fed up with ringing the bell. He rang it once to start with. He waited a good five minutes. He seems to have lost patience, as his finger presses the metal bell push for the umpteenth time.
Fatima comes rushing out of the kitchen, ready to open the door and scold the little joker.
But I stop her. I tell her he's a friend. She raises her eyes in exasperation. Trembling, I open the door for Alexandre. I don't say anything. I feel a bit emotional.
We go into the garden, which is on the other side of the house.
We lie down on the lawn. He takes my hand and holds it tightly. We close our eyes.
I haven't slept so peacefully since the night of the tragedy.
Alexandre left late in the afternoon. He kissed me on the forehead. I closed my eyes very tight to savour the moment, which left me feeling all dreamy.
Next day, at Théophile Gautier, Alexandre ignored me. I struggled to hold back the tears. Yet I was, to my great surprise, disconcertingly happy.

Paris

It's August. The heat is exhausting. The streets of the capital seem deserted. I feel as though I'm alone on Avenue Victor-Hugo, where household waste is piling up, giving off an unbearable stench of decay. The refuse collectors' strike has been wreaking havoc for two days now.
An hour ago I bought a ticket to Casablanca.
I haven't been back there for nearly twenty years.

It rained heavily in the night. Torrential summer rain. I didn't sleep a wink. Perhaps partly, too, because I'm anxious about going back to Morocco. It's as though I'd been bracketing off my childhood for years. Once I'd arrived in France, I'd never thought about my childhood in Casablanca again. I'd left it all over there, apart from a little scrap of white paper, folded in four, that I always keep with me.
Morning comes quickly.
I'm eager to reawaken the memories.

I haven't packed any suitcases. I've put the bare minimum in my bag. I couldn't be bothered. I'm not leaving. I'm going away and coming back. It isn't the same.
On my way to the airport, I think back to my arrival in Paris. I was happy that what lay ahead was unknown.
I was eighteen and I thought I'd seen it all. The years spent on the Côte d'Azur, where Mum and I had joined my father, had been incredibly calm. Stupefying. I thought the sluggishness of day-to-day

life had killed me. The only image that came to me of this time was of Mum lying on the bed, with a cigarette in her hand and a blank stare on her face. I struggled to get her attention; she was preoccupied by who knows what. She wasn't with me any more. She was in another world, and I didn't have the key.

As for my grandmother, she'd gone back to Poitou-Charentes, where she'd grown up. I almost lost track of her. Then, one weekend in Paris when I couldn't bear to be alone any longer, I took the train to Poitiers. I almost didn't recognise her. I don't think she was quite in her right mind any more.

We sat on the grass in the shade of some flowering snowball trees. We didn't mention Morocco. But we were thinking about it. The white flowers, lemons as big as grapefruit. The mint tea, burning hot, that I drank in little sips so that I could taste it better. The zellige-tiled fountain, with its water softly singing. Grandma had tears in her eyes. So I took her hand and squeezed it tight. I love my grandmother so much. But the next day I left her, alone in her garden, with its over-abundance of flowers.

The taxi is passing the Porte d'Orléans. I feel free. It's as though I were leaving behind everything that had been holding me in a world that isn't mine, to find my truth at last.

I felt the tiredness lift.

I put my hand absent-mindedly on my stomach. And I knew. In a panic, I told the taxi driver to turn back. I felt as though at any moment a rope was going to appear from nowhere and dangle me in the air.

Victor

Victor came into my life one October. It was overcast and the clatter of the packed Métro train was like a clichéd soundtrack for dull, grey days. I immediately noticed the blue eyes of the young man standing opposite me. He was smiling at me and flirted with me so blatantly that I felt a frisson of joy.
We filled the space between us with words, so as not to lose each other. Then he grabbed my hand. We'd gone past his station long ago. I was smiling. We got off at the next stop and wandered the streets of the capital until dawn. Paris had never seemed so radiant to me.

After that I experienced what I thought was happiness. I didn't want to be anywhere else. I just wanted to be there. Close to him. To wake up in the middle of the night just to watch him sleeping. To switch on the bedside lamp. And, in the shadowy half-light, study his body, abandoned to sleep, in this bed that was ours.
In the morning, he got up long before me and was astonished that I sleep so much. If only he'd known I'd spent a good part of the night just watching him sleeping, I wonder what he would have thought? He made me strong, hot coffee, just how I liked it. And he brought me brioches that he'd stopped to pick up when he went out to buy the newspaper. To me, these small things were acts of love.

It's morning. It's early. He wakes me with a kiss on the forehead. I see his face bathed in the light that's filtering through the half-open shutters.

He presses his eager body against mine.
He kisses the back of my neck.
I feel good.
His lips to my ear, I hear him whisper:
'I think I'm in love with you.'
My heart desired nothing more than this beautiful awakening.

Yesterday, Victor was out all day and I had nothing to do. I bought a copy of *L'Amour* by Marguerite Duras and settled down on the grass in the shade of a flowering plane tree opposite the Chalet des Îles. In the evening he came home later than usual. Very late. I had a whole list of complaints but, as soon as I saw him, I threw my arms around his neck and kissed him as hard as I could, as though I'd nearly lost him forever.

It's night-time. It's late. He isn't asleep.
Close to me. Not with me.
I'm scared.
I'm having difficulty breathing.
I'm afraid I'm not wrong.

I try to close the space between us.

I move my naked body closer to his.

He lies there as though he's dead.
He doesn't respond.

I put my lips close to his right ear. (I want to nibble his ear lobe, but I daren't.)
'I've been reading today.'
'What have you been reading?' Victor eventually asks.

'*L'Amour* by Marguerite Duras.'
'I don't much like Duras.'
'Oh, why not?'
'I don't know. I just don't.'
'Anyway, there's a passage that struck me.'
I wait.
His eyes are dead.
They don't respond.

So I go on:
'There's a married woman.
'Her husband is leaving her.
'She wants to know when he stopped loving her.
'"How long has it been going on?" she asks.
'He says, "Forever."'

Silence.

Faced with this cold composure, which is making my stomach churn,
I go on:
'Don't you think that's terrible?'

He said that's life.

I felt lost.

I try to close the space between us.

I place my bare lips against his.

His lips are dead.
They don't respond.

So I turned my back on him. I moved as far away from him as I could. Just to give him room to move closer.

It's morning. The bed is empty. Light is flowing across the room. I close the shutters because I'm afraid it might flow straight through my body.

Nan and Brian in Bed, New York, 1983

Yesterday I rang Luc again. I'd rather neglected him since Victor arrived on the scene. He's never held it against me. Perhaps that's what friendship is: understanding the other person's absence.
I think he knew straightaway, from my voice on the phone, that I wasn't feeling too good. He invited me to meet him at the Palais de Tokyo.
Wandering aimlessly along the wide marble walkways, we talked a lot, as though we were fearful that we'd almost lost each other.
My eye suddenly fell on a photograph. Luc, aware of my ignorance on the subject, said:
'*Nan and Brian in Bed*, New York, 1983. Nan Goldin. It's wonderful, isn't it?'
I thought it was rather sad, a man sitting on the edge of a bed, smoking a fag and seeming to ignore the woman behind him. She's watching him, looking as though she's both afraid and wants to move closer to him.
That's what I say to Luc.
He answers straight back:
'Different way of seeing it. Ah, the post-coital cigarette! It's a continuation of the pleasure. The pleasure of tobacco after the pleasure of the body.'
'You think they've just made love? She's wearing a black dress. Her

bare legs and the look on her face – they're looking for contact. I'm not convinced.'

'Who's talking about conviction? I'm talking about a subjective feeling, about the moment in the relationship when I want the photo to have been taken.'

'That's even more dismissive of her!'

'That's not what it's about. It's a continuation of the amorous embrace, but separately. Ask Victor what he thinks.'

I burst into tears. Luc listened to me, as he always did. He tried to reassure me. For the first time, he failed.

Victor told me he didn't love me any more one morning in November. The sky was icy blue and seemed to be sinking down into the city's narrow streets and alleys, where I was trying to shake off the evidence. I walked until the evening, but the dead space and cruel beauty of Paris just reminded me that I was alone again. I sat down on the steps of La Madeleine. I tried to think. My eyelids were heavy. Through moist eyes, I could just make out the shining lights of l'Opéra Garnier, which were like tiny will-o'-the-wisps smudged by my tears. Then the caretaker came along and chased me off. I couldn't see anything any more. I wandered around blindly for most of the night and then suddenly found myself back in front of Victor's apartment building. It was dawn. I sat on the pink marble steps in front of the main entrance. And I waited to catch sight of him. He was the only one who'd know what to do with me. I have no idea any more. I feel lost without him.

Casablanca

Dazzling whiteness. I go from one family to another, all with the same surname as my grandfather. I don't speak Arabic. I don't understand anything. The inability to communicate scrambles my brain. I'm terribly alone. A distant cousin of Grandpa's is watching me. Everyone calls him Uncle. He comes over to me. I feel as though he's listening to my heart. He holds his hand out to me. At last, someone is holding their hand out to me.
His hand isn't warm and reassuring like my grandfather's, even though the same blood runs in his veins. I want to pull my hand away. But I daren't.
We get into his big black Mercedes. He takes me to the biggest toyshop in the city. I'm spell-bound.

He said to me, 'Have whatever you want.'
I was stunned. I felt as though I was in a fairy tale, with all those toys holding their arms out to me. I wandered in a daze among all these things that could be mine, all mine. I was a nine-year-old girl again, with a child's heart.
I walk up the huge staircase in this temple of toys.
I falter suddenly.
I cling to the handrail.
I see my grandfather.
His hand slipping out of mine.
My hand hanging in empty space.

My grandfather's blood splashing onto the big white marble staircase.
I'm afraid of everything.
I hate all these toys.
My innocence has been stolen from me. I can't play any more. I've been damaged. I know I have. I'm scared of being killed.
I feel as though someone could take my life at any moment.
I open my eyes.
The glass eyes of a doll are looking at me. She wants me to save her. Perhaps she's scared as well, afraid that an innocent, thoughtless child will pull off her head. I take the doll. I decide to call her Louise.
I get back into the long black car with its tinted windows and it speeds off into the modern part of the city.

I went back to school. It was what Mum wanted. Everyone knows about the tragedy. I think it's obscene that the court case concerning Grandpa's death is still the main story in the Moroccan dailies. I feel as though I'm stripped naked in front of my school friends. It's unbearable. But even though they're young, they have the tact not to mention the subject. I don't know what Alexandre thinks of it. I'm happy to see him again. It's been such a long time.
Alexandre comes up to me. And he's the only one who dares say out loud what the others are whispering about.
'So, do they know who did it?'
'No.'
'It sounds as though it was your grandmother.'
Without knowing why, instead of telling him where to go, I break down with grief.
Alexandre goes on, 'She was there the night of the murder. So either she knows who did it, or it was her. And since she hasn't accused anyone…'
I start screaming. The teacher comes running towards me, waving his arms in the air to shoo Alexandre away.

'It's awful how cruel children can be to each other,' Mum says to my grandmother, whom I'd told about the incident at school.
I want to say, 'and not only to each other'. I know I've been cruel as well, to my grandmother. But I wanted to see her reaction: after all, I don't know if she's the one who killed Grandpa. I love her, but I want to know who my grandmother is. I see her differently now. Especially as she didn't give me a proper answer. She just said they were rumours. She didn't tell me they were lies. I'm going to keep my eyes peeled. I'm going to try to find out, even though I'd never give Grandma up to the police.

I sleep between Mum and Grandma. Her snoring doesn't drive me mad any more it reassures me. It tells me she's there. I know she's asleep. That she isn't up to anything else. Perhaps the enemy is here, now, in the bunker that my childhood bedroom has become. Tomorrow, they're going to reconstruct the crime. Grandma has decided to wait until tomorrow to reveal all. To disclose the unspeakable. Perhaps the unthinkable.
I'm so scared that the blood of a murderess might run in my veins. I look at the cut I made on my hand this morning. The blood still hasn't quite dried. I'm beginning to hate this blood, this hand, this body, which are mine. Which perhaps carry the genes of a murderer.

Mum bought me a packet of peanuts and we walked to the beach.
They're exactly the same as the ones my father gave me at the zoo in Saint-Jean-Cap-Ferrat to feed the animals, when they sent me to see him last summer.
They had the same beige-coloured shells, swollen at each end, which you had to break open to get at the nuts inside.

It was at the same zoo a few years earlier, when I'd just started nursery school, that my parents told me, amongst the giraffes with their long

necks, that love didn't last forever. They didn't love each other any more, but they would love me always.
A few weeks later, Mum and I moved to Morocco to live with my grandparents.

The beach is huge. The Atlantic is far away on the horizon. We wander along the shore. Mum is holding my hand. She is holding it tightly. As if she doesn't want it to get away. As if my hand was keeping her alive.
We lie down on the sand. Looking up at the silvery sky.
Mum tells me they used to come here, she and my father.
'People change, you know. One fine day I realised your father was no longer the man I'd met.'
I looked around. This must all be the same as it was when they came here years ago.
'At least things stay the same.'
'Yes,' Mum said quickly. 'But they no longer have the same meaning.'

Mum clasps my hand.
Our bodies are stretched out on the beach.
We close our eyes so that we melt into our seaside surroundings.
Mum's hand slackens. It opens a little and lets go of mine. Mum has fallen asleep.

I get up.
I'm opposite Sidi Abderrahmane.
The stone causeway is above the water.
I'm drawn towards the white limestone fortress.
I walk towards it.
I hear voices.
They are women's voices.
They are calling me.

It is a strange, ethereal sound.
Pure and clear.
I stop thinking.
It's as though I'm under a spell.
Possessed.
I walk towards Sidi Abderrahmane.
The water is rising.
Suddenly, I hear a sharp cry cutting through the air.
I look around.
Mum has got up and is coming towards me.
I turn around.
As we walk back, Mum doesn't say a word.
She was holding my hand so tightly that it hurt.
She was walking so fast that my body, which she was dragging along with her, struggled to keep up.

When we got back to Mira Ventos, she explained to me.
Nobody knows what goes on at Sidi Abderrahmane.
The women who get away from there are no longer quite in their right mind. It's as if only their bodies have come back, leaving their souls behind. Often, a little while later, they're found to be pregnant. That's why, for thousands of years, women who can't have children have been going there. They know very well that they will lose their souls, but they prefer that to the public shame of not giving their husband an heir.
Nobody knows what goes on at Sidi Abderrahmane.
People prefer not to know.

We were expecting Albert and Geneviève Pilot for lunch.
At eleven o'clock the phone rang and Fatima removed two place settings from the big rectangular table.
People think that other people's misfortune is catching. Albert Pilot

was a friend of my grandparents. A famous artist known for his paintings of Morocco. But the painting my grandfather had wanted to have at Mira Ventos was *Les Champs-Élysées sous la pluie*. For him, it was about hanging a little bit of France on his wall – the wall of a Spanish-style villa in Morocco.

The Madness Stone[*]

I spent all morning waiting on the freezing steps in front of Victor's apartment building. In full view of staring passers-by, who looked me up and down as though I was an animal at market. The main door opened several times; I had my back to it, and I could feel my heart beating wildly every time I heard footsteps approaching. I jumped every time the wide oak door creaked on its hinges.
Instant disappointment every time. I was sweating. It was very hot. The sun was at its highest point, crushing down on me, when I saw Victor at the corner of the street. He was strolling along, without a care in the world.
He looked so immaculate, so perfect, incredibly calm. Then he spotted me. His face fell and took on a devastating look of contempt. I knew straightaway that if I wanted to keep the little bit of dignity I had left, then all I could do was walk away. I didn't move. What if I was wrong? What if I was misreading things?
He was right beside me.
As calm as anything, he said, 'I never want to hear of you again. Go away. You disgust me.'
I wanted something from him. Even if it was only his pity.
But he carried on walking and left me, gaping, in the emptiness of a street packed with office workers from Avenue Victor-Hugo on their lunch break.

---

[*]Allusion to the untranslated poetry collection of the same name (*La pierre de la folie*) by Fernando Arrabal.

I shut myself away in my flat. I didn't want to be alive any more. I didn't understand anything any more. It felt like a nightmare.
One day, I don't know if it was in the morning or the evening, someone knocked at the door. I rose from the dead. I wanted to take my time before answering. I didn't want Victor to see I'd been devastated by him, that he had power over me. Victor likes strong women. Women who don't need anyone. I just need him. I splash my face with water. I don't recognise myself in the mirror. My face is thin and drawn. I look ten years older. Now I don't want to open the door. I'll go and see him at his place.
I'm diving back under the sweaty duvet when I hear Luc's voice. Instant disappointment. I run to open the door.

Luc is worried. He wants me to see a doctor. I can't eat anything. But not because I don't want to. It's my body that doesn't want to. Luc feeds me with a teaspoon like a baby. I regain a little strength. My spirits lift a little. But, as soon as I feel stronger, I start thinking again. I don't want to think any more. As soon as I start thinking, I think about him.

Luc has a working dinner. It's late. I'm scared at night. I've always been scared. With Victor's arms around me, I'd felt safe. I'd felt loved.
Alone in the room, I spot Luc's house phone. I realise Victor might answer if he doesn't think it's me again.
I dial Victor's number. It rings.
I'm scared. Scared of his reaction. Anyway, if he doesn't pick up, I'll try again from another number he doesn't recognise.
Someone answers.
I hear his voice.
I feel as though I'm about to faint with emotion.
I stammer and then manage to say, 'When did you stop loving me? How long has it been going on?'

'Forever.'

I hear him hang up.

The sad sound of the telephone is washed up in the void. I'm alone, clinging to a rock with empty space spinning around me.

I wanted to forget everything. But can you wipe out your past? I tried anyway.

I began by emptying my small flat, which I'd gone back to when Victor and I split up.

I threw everything away. Everything I'd accumulated over the years. Anything that might remind me of a previous existence. Start from scratch.

My effort was in vain. Especially with the refuse collectors' strike beginning the very day of my resurrection. I could see them all the time, outside the door of the building, my precious memories amidst the rubbish. Then all I wanted to do was to save the remnants of my past from my neighbours' food waste. I couldn't bear it any longer. The only answer was to go back to Casablanca as soon as possible.

The days pass. I don't want to see anyone. I want to disappear myself. Forget everything. 'Confuse all.'* Change everything about. I can't even bear my own presence.

Someone knocks at the door. I don't answer.

They knock again. I still don't answer.

Last night, when I got back from the airport, two pink lines on a little bit of plastic confirmed that I was pregnant.

I felt eternity swinging in the void.

Rain covers my bedroom windows with endless rivulets of water. It's cold outside. Inside too. I wrap myself in a big white synthetic duvet. I'm still cold. I touch my stomach, which hasn't changed but which holds the possibility of a human being. I curl up. I feel warmer already.

---

*Quotation from 'Perdre le Midi quotidien' by Victor Segalen.

But the cold starts to take over again. I clasp my icy feet in forlorn hands. I'm cold again.
Oh, for an end to the agonising sound of the rain. That vague, nagging moan seeping into the bedroom.
I feel so alone. Curl up as tight as possible. It doesn't do any good. I'm no good.
Tears run down the bedroom windows. I feel them spilling down my face.
Empty hours stretch to the horizon. I can hear the silence – the silence that had reigned over my life ever since we left Morocco, and which had come to an end with Victor.
It's back. I can't bear it any more. I can hear it. It's deafening me. I put my hands over my ears so I can't hear the emptiness sucking me in.
The rain turns into drizzle. A low, grey sky. The silence getting louder. My stomach getting heavier.

I don't want to go to Casablanca any more, or anywhere else. I want to find Victor. I can't get him out of my mind.
I walked to Avenue Victor-Hugo, my stomach heavy with broken promises.
The front door was open.
Standing outside Victor's door, I didn't know what I was going to say.
I knocked gently, then louder.
The concierge appeared.
'He isn't here any more. He's moved. He's living in Marseille now.'
He gave me the forwarding address.
I went to the Gare de Lyon and bought a ticket for Marseille.
I killed time among the wavering mirrors of Le Train Bleu restaurant, where I kept seeing the reflection of a face that was just like mine, but with an expression of long-suffering sadness that I hated.
Someone gave me a mint cordial. The stranger said I looked sad.
The Le Train Bleu waiter walks away and I try to smile. The mirrors show

me a dead face wearing a forced smile. I think of my empty seat on the plane leaving for Casablanca and I feel a mixture of hope and despair.

I'm at Gare Saint-Charles, Marseille. I'm lost. A taxi takes me to the Corniche. It's beautiful. It's a cliff towering above the sea. I'm struck by the beauty of the small limestone island rising above the churning water, which I learned later is called Château d'If. The window is wide open. The Mistral wind is definitely not a myth.

A building on the seafront. The main door is open. I go up to the top floor and knock at the door. To my amazement, the door opens and Victor is there, unbelievably, right in front of me. Pathetically, I tell him in a flat voice that I'm expecting his child.
Victor's face falls.
Then he smiles.
'I'll help you.'
His words ring in my head, a sudden burst of hope.

He tucks me up in his bed. The sheets smell lovely. He's gentle, like he used to be. He kisses me on the lips. I'm so reassured that, after all the nights of insomnia, I fall into a deep sleep.

I wake up feeling as though I've been asleep for years.
Victor's eyes are hard again.
He takes me to the doctor.
We buy some pills that I reluctantly agree to take.
As I lie looking out over the Frioul archipelago, its shores lapped by a calm sea, I feel happiness leaving me forever.
I'm bleeding. I feel as though my insides are falling out.
I took a look before throwing it all into the dustbin. And I saw this sticky red thing, which looked as though it had eyes. I screamed.
Victor came and told me to think of the neighbours.

I wanted to show him the thing. He didn't want to look.
I put this small slimy creature in an old tin tea caddy, and we went out onto the rocks.
Victor took the caddy out of my hands and threw it into the sea.
It didn't sink.
So he picked up some stones and threw them at it, but it still didn't sink, even though he was a good shot.
He seemed to think it was funny.
I just wanted to push him onto the rocks.

I went back to Paris, where the refuse collectors' strike was getting worse.
I stayed for one night. Next morning I found myself back on the train to Marseille. I could feel that ball of living flesh in my belly, though I knew it was in the sea. I had to go back to the place my shattered life had left me chained to. The place where hell had got into my head. Where the suffering of my soul had broken free of space and time, leaving me no respite.
Back to the insomnia haunted by memories, delving deep into the scheme of things, so that I could understand. Find the key and realise that happiness is there, beneath the human scum. Cleanse it all away, to be reborn at last.

I was outside the door, waiting for Victor. A neighbour came home. I slipped into the lair.
I sat waiting a few steps down, from where, hidden in the shadowy half-light, I could see the front door opening, letting in shadows that lengthened as they went up the spiral staircase.
I watched the shadows pass. I could smell them. I heard shouts, voices, whispers.
I was part of the building and I was beginning to realise how much life teemed behind this concrete façade on Avenue Kennedy.

Victor came home in the middle of the night. I jumped up and ran towards him.
He grabbed me by the hands and shouted for someone to call the police.
The police came and put shiny silver handcuffs on my wrists.
Two policemen drove me back to the railway station.
'There's no law against being a bastard to a woman,' one of them said.
I didn't answer.
He gave me a kind look and they left.
I waited for the first train in the morning, but I didn't take it. I could feel the anger growing inside me. Get Mum's revolver. Wait for Victor inside his apartment building. Shoot him.
I wanted to kill Victor.
He killed my child, the child of our love-making.
All bound together in the sea. Words of love in a pulp of viscous flesh. He had no right. I wandered around Marseille, wondering how I could get hold of a revolver.
Night was falling. The statue of David was bathed in a pool of golden light whose beauty made me shiver. I felt as though I was no longer quite right in the head, because of Victor. As though I'd never again feel uplifted by the beauty of the world around me. The sun bathing everything in a tawny orange light. The statue of David. The sea. A ball of flesh in the water. What this child might have been. Holding it in my arms. Soft, pink skin. Innocent eyes. I would have given my life for this child.
Find the hiding place. Take Mum's pistol. Shoot. The sound of the redeeming shot. Throwing Victor's body into the sea. Not leaving the child all alone. Then joining them beneath the water myself.

Night had fallen, gently. I knocked at a door. An Arab woman opened it. I asked for a screwdriver. She called her husband. He gave me one without asking any questions. I must have looked like a lost soul.

Someone went into Victor's apartment building. I followed him in. I went up the stairs to the top floor with a feigned confidence in my step, a bit like a soldier setting off for battle not knowing what the outcome will be.

Victor's door. I stop breathing so I can hear better. I thought I could hear moaning. I could hear it only very faintly. It must be coming from the bedroom.

They were the moans of a young woman. I was sure of it. She was moaning with pleasure.

Victor inside her. The body of a woman who wasn't me. Victor's body. Both of them naked. Making love.

Embracing. Entwined together.

The smell of Victor.

Victor's body. My naked body. Victor inside me. I moan with pleasure. Victor whispering in my ear, 'I think I'm in love with you.'

I hear the young woman orgasm. An unbearable reality that hits me full in the face. I take the screwdriver and try to open the lock. I fail. Cries of pleasure. Victor's body on top of hers. I force the door with the screwdriver. It gives a little.

I try harder. I still can't open it.

Louder cries. I can hear Victor coming in her.

I'm going to smash the door in.

Suddenly I hear a voice behind me.

It's Victor.

Quietly and contemptuously, he says, 'Poor little lunatic. You're trapped. I've called the police.'

I wanted to leave. He wouldn't let me. I tried to touch him, so he'd remember how much he enjoyed my body, how intoxicating he found it.

He became violent and pushed me down the stairs.

The police arrived. Suddenly there were shiny silver handcuffs on my wrists.

I couldn't walk. My left leg hurt.
Night at the police station.
Eyes swollen with tears.
The next day I was questioned. I think the female superintendent felt sorry for me.
They told me to leave. I asked if they were going to take me somewhere. They said I was free to go and that I'd have to make my own way home. I had difficulty finding the railway station.
In despair, I took the first train to Paris.
I could feel my skin quivering and my heart struggling, as if my soul was fleeing my body, leaving an icy trail behind it, leaving me to become a lifeless, aimless shadow, drowning in misery.

Back in Paris, I went home and slept until the evening.
When I woke up, I felt utterly lost. At first I thought I'd stay in the tear-soaked bed until someone found my body there, dead from grief.
Outside it's raining very hard. I look out of the window. You can't see anything except the rain. I open the window. I hold my hand out under the morning cloudburst.
When it rained in Morocco it was like that, torrential. I didn't like it, I didn't like getting soaked to the skin. Drenched. I didn't want to go outside any more. One rainy morning, my grandfather had come to find me. He'd smiled at me. Then he'd talked to me about the magic of rain. Told me that it was so rare in Morocco that farmers prayed for it. And when it began to thunder in the distance, they'd go out and dance in the rain to give thanks to the sky. My grandfather had taken my hand and led me out into the garden. Then he'd twirled me round and round until the storm came to an end.
He laughed and laughed, and now I loved the rain.
I draw my hand back inside. The floor is sopping wet. I love this invasion of the inside by the outside.
I remember just how my grandfather's warm hand felt in mine.

I remember something my grandfather had said to Mum when we went back to live in Morocco after she left my father: 'Life is not about waiting for the storm to pass; it's about learning to dance in the rain.'
My grandfather's gentle smile.
Mum, who had agreed to stop mourning her carefree youth.
My grandfather who, far from disowning her, was proud of his daughter.
That look, in which you can see the love for the beloved.
I have to rediscover the will to live.
I left the window wide open, while it went on and on raining, and I booked a seat on the next morning's plane to Casablanca.

In the plane, I kept thinking about Victor's behaviour. I was beginning to realise that you could utterly despise someone whilst still loving them to death.

Allahu Akbar

Louise and I are watching what's going on around us. The house has been cordoned off, for the reconstruction of the crime. The whole neighbourhood is crawling with police and strung about with red and yellow tape.

There's a lot of noise. Everyone's rushing about. Grandma is going to play the part of herself. Uncle is going to take Grandpa's place. And policemen are going to be the criminals.

A few hours later, everyone's crowding around wanting to know what happened, according to my grandmother. Mum's in such a state of shock that she's left Mira Ventos. I think she's forgotten about me.

The policemen re-enact the criminals' crude behaviour, the way they'd broken the furniture and slashed the Persian carpet, which still lies in tatters in the entrance hall.

I see my grandfather, probably alerted by all the noise, coming down the white marble staircase.

One of the hooded men has already gone upstairs. Standing behind my grandfather, who doesn't know he's there, he pushes him down the white marble staircase, where his head hits the stone.

Then he hit Grandpa over the head with the bust of Juba, which was found covered in blood.

Grandma's in the bedroom. Another hooded man went to find her.

She pretended to be dead.

He hesitated. He knew she was still alive.

She opened her eyes.

She said, 'Allahu Akbar' (God is Great).
The man left her alone then. She heard him shouting to the others that the job was done.
I was terrified. I believed my grandmother. I was instantly ashamed of having suspected her. I can hear people around me saying it's a bit far-fetched.
But I'm sure my grandmother's telling the truth.
I look at Louise. Her eyes look dead. She doesn't seem to care that I'm distressed.
I press my hands hard against her throat. As if I'm going to choke her. She still doesn't care. So I tug hard on her head. I'm so upset. Her head comes off. I run crying to Grandma, because my doll is broken.

Grandma is in the study. The door is ajar. She's talking and talking. I can't make sense of the racket coming through the half-open door. I'm curious to know who's with her.
I walk towards the door. I glance at the chair opposite her. It's empty. Grandma is on her own, jabbering some endless, unintelligible refrain.
I walk towards her. She looks at me as though she has a secret. She gestures for me to sit down.
Her eyes bulging, she says, 'I know who did it.'
I wait, feeling rather stunned.
'I know who did it.'
'Who?' I ask eagerly.
'The government,' she whispers.
'It's the government,' she goes on. 'They're probably bugging us. Be careful. We're going on a journey. Running away. I'm sure they want us dead, too.'
I don't understand. I can't see what connection my grandfather might have with the government.
She tells me to leave her alone.
I run off to throw a few things in a bag.

I spent the rest of the day examining every nook and cranny at Mira Ventos.
I didn't find anything. The mikes must be well hidden.

Prayer for the Dead

Uncle has come back to fetch me. I have to go and sleep at his house. The haughtiness of the other day has gone and he has a worried look on his face. On the way, he looks out of the window as his driver takes a detour along the edge of the sea. The Mercedes stops. There are gaps in the thick spray thrown up by the raging sea.

In the distance, you can see Sidi Abderrahmane.

Uncle gets out of the car. He walks along the shore. I get out to follow him but the driver signals to me to stay where I am.

Uncle disappears in the fog. The tide is starting to go out and the mist is clearing. The seagulls are agitated. They're like crazy things. You can't hear the sea now. Just the seagulls' piercing cries. You can't tell whether they're laughing or howling. Some of them fly round and round until they must be dizzy, and then come down to stand motionless on the waterlogged sand, which is as hard as rock. It feels as though you've travelled back in time. Rocks are emerging from the sea, so you can reach Sidi Abderrahmane on foot.

Utter silence. Some women are walking across to Sidi Abderrahmane. They are faceless women. Bodies that are swallowed up by the huge island of white limestone. Bloodless lamentations ring out along the shore. It is a sanctuary for lost souls.

I'm scared. I want to leave. The driver is standing right by the car, staring into the distance.

He's watching the cortège of women walking away from the shore. I want to ask him if we can leave. When Uncle will come back. But he

doesn't understand French. Uncle is the only one who speaks it. I think that's why he was asked to look after me.
The tide is starting to come in. The seagulls are motionless. They are watching. The sea is turning the huge dune into a thin, pathetic strip of filthy sand.
The Atlantic has reclaimed its sovereignty. You can see the seagulls flying out to sea. They're incredibly calm. Without a care in the world, like people who've never known hell. I almost envy them.
Then I remember what happened earlier. They have just escaped death. The seagulls on the ground have been carried away forever by the vastness of the sea that is washing up in foaming waves at my feet. It's as though nothing had happened and everything was beginning again. The seagulls' light-heartedness seems cruel to me now. I feel sick.
The mist has returned. Uncle's long black coat appears in the distance. He's walking towards us. He doesn't look at me. He gets into the car. He doesn't seem worried any more. He signals to the driver to go. He closes his eyes. He instantly falls asleep.
The car drives along the shore. In the mist, I spot the clown of Casablanca, whose wild eyes follow the black saloon as it drives away and disappears in the exhaust smoke of the cars travelling along the boulevard that leads into the city.
A human figure stuck to the pot-holed tarmac of the road that runs along the edge of the sea.
As though fixed forever in the landscape of the shore of Sidi Abderrahmane.
As though determined to be nothing more than an image.
The sad look that suddenly appears on her face makes her sublime.
She is a prisoner to her grief.

I've been at Uncle's house for several days and I'm bored. There are lots of people who speak only Arabic. Uncle is hardly ever there. I spend the whole day waiting for him to come home.

One evening he comes to me and says:

'Would you like us to go and fetch your doll?'

'No, she's dead.'

Uncle looks me up and down.

He doesn't understand.

He tells me what I already know:

'You can only die if you've been alive. She must be broken, that's all. We can mend her if you like.'

'No, I don't want to.'

'Then we'll go and get another one tomorrow.'

'No, I don't want to.'

'Why not?'

'I don't know.'

Exasperated, Uncle walks out of the kitchen, which is where I've taken refuge, and leaves me there among the cooks who are preparing tajines for tomorrow.

It's odd, but I'm relieved he's gone.

I think I did it on purpose.

Uncle's driver takes me home. I'm happy.

I ring the doorbell with an eagerness I can barely contain.

Mum opens the door. I wrap my arms tight around her. I've missed her so much.

Down the hallway, I can see Grandma smiling at me.

It's good to be together again at last, the three of us.

Grandma has made a tajine with prunes. It's my favourite. But it doesn't taste the same as usual. There's something missing. You can't taste the saffron. And there aren't any sesame seeds on top. Of course, Fatima usually makes it. But where is Fatima?

I ask. Mum and Grandma don't say a word. I ask again. This time they look at each other.

In the end Grandma answers:
'Fatima's gone. She handed in her notice. Your grandfather's murder has frightened her.'
I don't say anything. You can feel the tension. The tragedy I've experienced makes me feel like a pariah.
I realise I mustn't talk about this part of my life, which will affect me forever.
Yesterday, the police rang at the door. They took Hassan away. He didn't say anything. They secured his hands behind his back with shiny silver handcuffs.
Hassan looked at me as he was leaving. For the first time, I saw hatred in his eyes.

Newspapers are piled up in a jumble on the dining-room table. They're all talking about Grandpa's death.
I don't want to see what's inside. I'm afraid to know.

Fatima and Hassan gone.
The house empty.
White marble still stained with blood.
Torn carpets.
Les Champs-Élysées by Albert Pilot on the main wall.
A huge ceiling.
The smallest room on the first floor.
Mum, Grandma and me.
Kitchen knives and a saucepan under the mattress.
The door double-locked.
The moon is full. You can see it through the slits in the shutters. You'd have to nail boards against the windows to be any safer.

This evening, it's the execution.
The newspapers talk of nothing else. Now I read them all. I even help Grandma make a scrapbook. The blade cuts my grandfather's story, the story of his death, out of the rest of life.
We know pretty much what happened now.
Fatima and Hassan.
Yet no stolen glances.
Yet lovers despite the age difference.
Two builders who worked for Uncle's firm.
Fatima unlocked the door in the middle of the night.
She knew.
How could she look at me, smile at me, talk to me, when she knew she was going to shatter my family's life forever?
How could she?
I try to remember. I can't remember anything that might have given her away.
I can see her bringing mint tea. I can hear her telling me she loves me as if I were her own daughter. I can still feel her hand stroking my hair.
I want to scream.

Fatima is part of the story of Mira Ventos. My grandfather had just finished his medical training in Bordeaux and had brought my grandmother back to Morocco with him. They bought Mira Ventos very soon after they arrived, from a thin Spanish woman ravaged by time. They liked the name: Mira Ventos, Facing the Wind. It was partly what decided them. They took on Fatima, who'd recently started working for the old woman.
Hassan came to Mira Ventos much later. Grandpa had had a row with the caretaker. He'd asked Rachid to sweep up the dead leaves. The next day my grandfather said to him: 'Rachid, you haven't swept up the leaves.' Rachid had replied: 'What's the point, when there'll be more down tomorrow?'

So Grandpa had gone out into the countryside and had found a fairly fit man of about sixty at the side of the road. 'A real country man,' he'd said. 'You don't find men like that any more.'
Hassan had moved into the little white-limestone house at the bottom of the garden that very evening.

Yesterday I walked past Hassan's house. It's behind the bougainvillea Grandpa was so proud of. The door is made of carved wooden latticework. It's imposing. Impressive. Despite the vice gripping my heart, I pushed it open.
The police have already been here in any case.
The door had been sealed until the end of the court case. It was re-opened the morning of the verdict.
It's rather grubby. A mattress lies on the bare floor. The limestone walls are covered with a layer of grime. It clashes with the beauty of Mira Ventos. Lots of books in Arabic are strewn across the floor. There's a copy of the Quran. The place stinks of hashish and fanaticism.
I realised that Hassan and Fatima lived with us in appearance only. They had their own separate life. I regretted not showing more interest in them, having failed to soften their hearts so they might have spared my grandfather.
The image of Hassan and me raiding the fruit trees comes back to me. I feel sick.

Fatima had used the copies of the keys to Mira Ventos that had been entrusted to her to open the door for the murderers.
It was Hassan who'd asked her to do it.
They entered the house. They wrecked everything. They took the bust of Juba II that was prominently displayed in the entrance hall. They thought it was a bust of Christ. When Hassan joined them, also hooded, they gave it to him. Alerted by all the noise, Grandpa came down the stairs.

Hassan, who'd already gone up to the first floor, hit Grandpa on the head with the bronze 'Christ'.
That's how they found the bust of Juba II, King of Mauritania – covered in blood, next to my grandfather's body.

One gunshot.
Allahu Akbar
Two gunshots.
Allahu Akbar
Three gunshots.
Allahu Akbar
Plus a life sentence for Fatima, who was released five years later.

The delirious crowd chants the greatness of God.
People flock to public executions.
They killed for God. They didn't say anything else. They said Grandpa had a statue of Christ. That he was a heretic.

Grandma's book, *Moi, Juba roi de Maurétanie*, came out soon after the execution. The bust of Juba was on the front cover. Grandma had had the photo taken especially.

Grandpa's murderers are dead. The two builders gave themselves up to the police and told them what had happened. They didn't say anything else. We still don't know whether the crime was commissioned. But we think so. All Hassan's books, all the drugs found at the murderers' homes. They couldn't afford any of that. And to turn themselves in, that seems really odd. They were executed. We never learned anything more. Grandpa is dead. Dead forever, and nothing can bring him back.

One gunshot

Two gunshots
Three gunshots
fired in the air

The house has been cordoned off.

Grandpa's body is lying on the white marble staircase.

The body is carried away.
The men of the family leave with the body.

Uncle decided he'd take care of everything.

Upstairs, my grandfather's body is laid out in my grandparents' bedroom. I'm not allowed in. I'm told Grandpa is going to be wrapped in a white shroud.
The imam arrives.

Amidst the weeping of the women, in the distance you can hear the voice of the imam, followed by the voices of the men of the family:
'La ilaha illa illa-ilah'
(There is no god but God)
'Muhammadan rasul ullah'
(Muhammad is the messenger of God)

Then the body was carried away.
The cortège of men, led by Uncle, returns at dusk.
Grandpa is dead and buried forever.
Tomorrow, we shall go to the cemetery.

The cemetery – le cimetière des Martyrs. The family burial plot. We bought warm bread for the beggars.

We'd walked only a little way before it was all gone.
Grandma bends down to pick up three handfuls of sand, which she throws onto Grandpa's grave.
She hands the coin to an old man dressed in white.
We can hear the Prayer for the Dead.

Nan

New York, 1983.
Nan puts her camera on a metal tripod.
She sets the automatic shutter-release.
She doesn't know when the photo will be taken.

Zoé, Roger and Elsa

'Go to sleep, my child. Sleep now.'
Mum is with me.
The big clock brought back from France chimes seven o'clock.
She strokes my hair. At last I fall asleep.

My grandfather wakes me.
It is dawn.
He's taking me out with him.
'As quick as you can,' he says to me. 'While we can still see the morning dew beading the blooms on the rose bushes.'
First we do a grand tour of the garden. He shows Hassan what he has to do today. Then he fetches a wicker basket from the kitchen and borrows Grandma's car to go to the market.
There are so many smells. Some of them lovely. Others unfamiliar. Cumin. Perfumed spices. The smell of poultry being butchered. The cries of sheep. And birds. Parakeets. Rabbits with long bodies like Roger Rabbit. Tortoises. The stall-holder takes my index finger and places it on the latticed dome of one of their shells. I stroke it and the tortoise's head disappears inside. I laugh. My grandfather hands over five dirhams: Zoé is mine!

Yesterday my grandfather wasn't quite himself. He seemed worried. I didn't understand.
Uncle had been to see him and had left behind a black briefcase with

a gold combination lock. I tried lots of combinations, just for fun, but also because I wanted to know what was inside.
I waved it about.
I shook it. It didn't make a sound. Then I chucked it on the floor, but Grandpa came in and slapped me. I cried. He said he was sorry. I was cross and went upstairs to find Mum.

The atmosphere at Mira Ventos has changed. You can feel the tension. My grandfather doesn't smile any more. Fatima goes to the market to do the shopping and Grandpa stays in bed very late. He isn't even going to his surgery any more.
The black briefcase is in the study now. I'm not allowed in there. Grandpa has locked the door. He keeps the key in his pocket all the time. I've watched out for a chance to get hold of it. But he's very careful.

I cried a lot last night because Zoé has disappeared. Grandpa got up early this morning and went to the market with Fatima. He brought Roger back for me. He's a huge rabbit with long, dangling ears that I try to tie in a knot to make a pretty headband for him.

This morning, Alexandre invited me to go to Tahiti Beach. It's a big swimming pool on the beachfront where you can pig out on cornets filled with vanilla, strawberry or pistachio ice cream.
I was really looking forward to it. But when I got there, there were other friends of Alexandre's there as well. They teased me the whole time. I couldn't wait for the longed-for day to come to an end.

When I got home, supper was ready. The meat was much more tender than mutton. I asked Fatima what it was. She told me it was rabbit.

I searched everywhere for Roger. I went crazy looking for him. Grandpa came to find me and said he'd sent him to stay at a farm in the country. I pretended to believe him, because my grandfather isn't himself at the moment. But he knows me. He knows I know we've eaten Roger.

And after Roger there was Elsa the parakeet, who arrived in a blue and white cage.

Victor

I've taken a room on the shore facing Sidi Abderrahmane. It's night-time. I've just woken up. I'm not in Paris. I'm not in the flat on Avenue Victor-Hugo. I'm not with Victor. The bed is empty. The sheets don't smell of him any more. But I imagine the smell of him all the time. I know its undertones. I know you so much better than you know yourself, Victor. I could recreate you exactly.

I can see Sidi Abderrahmane, a dark shape against the horizon. It is lighter now. I'm the only person awake. I'd like to go back to sleep forever. I wish I'd never woken up. Yes, I'd like to have stopped breathing just before he abandoned me.
Die with a smile on my face. Not know. Still believe.
Why didn't you stop my breath just before you left, Victor?
Why didn't you put your fingers around my throat and squeeze hard?
It would have been so easy. Everything would've been easier.
I wouldn't be struggling to live now.

Grandpa is Dead

Geneviève and Albert Pilot have just arrived for lunch. My grandmother has taken bottles of spirits out of a carefully-locked cupboard.
My grandmother likes whisky. She drinks it any time of the day. My grandfather doesn't drink alcohol.
The painter is talking a lot, as usual. They all go out into the garden for lunch.
The smell of spices and marinated peppers. Lamb's brain served in small bowls.
Then a tajine à la française. Followed by mint tea and delicious pastries filled with honey that burst in your mouth.
The painter has spent the whole time talking about his love of Morocco. Of the light that is like nowhere else.

The water in the zellige-tiled fountain dancing in the air. Palm trees a hundred years old. My white house. The sun. How beautiful the light is! Magical.
Then Albert starts talking about his son, Henri. He's sad because he's ill. He has schizophrenia.
He doesn't know what to do. My grandfather strokes his friend's shoulder.
He tells him the French word for madness, 'la folie', comes from the Greek and used to mean balloons that you inflated and which floated away on the breeze.

The painter said he liked that image.
I think he smiled.
They all started laughing again.

Elsa has opened her cage. She seems to have gone mad. She's flying round and round the living room. She's banging into the walls, covering them with claw marks. Then her warm body falls stone dead on the cold white marble.
Fatima told me it was a bad omen.

The tension is even more palpable at supper. The meal passes in a terrifying silence. Nobody bothers to liven things up. Grandpa goes off to bed before dessert. Mum and Grandma don't touch it. I'm a little ashamed to take another plateful of beghir, Moroccan pancakes, drizzled with honey.

The next day, Mum tells me she's taking me on holiday. I know it's to get me away. We're going to Marrakech, Oualidia and then Tangier, to Le Mirage Hotel.

After two days in Marrakech, in a shabby hotel where Moroccan boys share rooms with much older European men, Mum decided we were going to Oualidia.
In the hotel restaurant, looking out over a pink sea pleated by sand dunes, the head waiter hurried over to my mother as we were fiddling with sea urchins.
Mum went out into the lobby. I waited for more than an hour. Then the head waiter came to get me.
Grandpa is dead.

The house has been sold to the CEO of a big German company. Deutschmarks are piled up in a jumble on the cold white marble at Mira Ventos.
We're leaving for France soon.
Mum and Grandma are getting ready for their return. For me, it's a departure, or rather the end of a life, my life as a child.

A Frenchman came to collect the deutschmarks. In exchange he gave Grandma a French cheque with lots of zeros. I was entrusted with it. Grandma told Mum that nobody would ever frisk a young girl. I slipped it against the straight, jutting bone of my hip, just under my knicker elastic.

Yesterday the police came and questioned Grandma. She didn't want to tell me anything. We have to leave in twenty-one days precisely. I can see Grandma's afraid.
I suddenly remember Uncle's black briefcase. I ask Grandma where it is. She tells me he came to fetch it the very morning of the murder.

Black night.
The nursery.
Mum, Grandma and me.
Mum jumps and whispers in terror.
There's someone in the house.
Grandma tells her not to do anything.
She gets the revolver.
We can hear footsteps in the living room.
My grandmother tells her not to make a sound. Not to leave the room.

That's what cost Grandpa his life.
Mum is like her father.
She leaves the room.
One gunshot. We hear a man's voice cry out in pain.
A short silence.
Two gunshots. More cries of pain.
Whispering.
Three gunshots. Silence.
Mum comes back. She looks like a madwoman. With rolling eyes, she declaims, 'I got him! I'll get them all, Papa! Do you hear me?'
She's very upset.
Grandma puts a pill in her mouth and raises a glass of water to her lips to help her swallow it.
We look at the dead man's face. We don't know who he is. He looks like a tramp.
Mum is sobbing. Grandma takes her back into the bedroom. I follow them because I don't want to be on my own with the body. Grandma tucks Mum up in bed and tells her not to worry, she'll deal with everything. Then she looks at me apologetically. 'We don't have much time.'
Together we dragged the body out into the garden and pushed it down the well.
We heard the thud of a heavy weight falling into deep water.
Grandma took me back to Mum, who had fallen asleep.
She put the revolver in a little hiding place by the bed.
She went to clean up. And I was ready to jump up and grab the revolver at the slightest suspicious sound.

In the morning, Grandma told me we were going off on a trip around the country before leaving. We dropped Mum off at a nursing home in the middle of nowhere.
There's nothing left at Mira Ventos. All the furniture has already been

sold. The only things left are the bed in the nursery and *Les Champs-Élysées sous la pluie.*

Le Mirage Hotel.
I'm walking along the edge of the water.
Yesterday, the Yale choir left.
I dig my bare feet into the sand.
A deflated balloon has washed up on the beach.
It's the same colour as the one Alexandre had launched into the air.

It's our last night before leaving.
'Just tonight and we're home and dry,' Grandma whispers to Mum.

I can't sleep.
In the middle of the night, I hear noises.
Someone's ringing the doorbell. Grandma looks out through the slits in the shutters. It's the police.
They force the front door.
They put shiny silver handcuffs on my grandmother and take her away.
Mum looks at me anxiously.
Once the police have gone, she whispers in my ear, 'Who could have informed on your grandmother? We have to be careful. They might be bugging us.'

It was several days before Grandma came home.
Mum was scared they'd forced Grandma to confess.
She told me about a time when Rachid had disappeared and Grandpa had gone to fetch him at the prison. He'd found him there, covered in bruises. The physical pain inflicted on him was so unbearable that he'd confessed to committing a robbery.
Mum went on to say she didn't understand why they'd been so quick

to execute her father's murderers. They should have been as determined as they'd been with our old gardener. On the day of the execution, they didn't look as though they'd been mistreated. They should have got more information out of them. Everyone believed they were nothing more than pawns, and that the person who'd commissioned the crime was perhaps living amongst us. They should have waited before killing them.

'And what about Fatima?' I asked, full of hope.

'Her brother's in the police. Untouchable. You'll see, in a few years' time you might well bump into her in the street.'

A mixture of anger and fear swept over me.

One morning in November, we heard they'd thrown the CEO out of the country and seized all his assets. Grandma came home the next morning. She confessed to the police. She'd apparently told them everything the day she was arrested. She'd talked only about what she'd been accused of, which was tax fraud.

So we took the plane to France. Pilot's painting was the only thing we took with us.

Grandma and Mum can't go back to Morocco until they're sixty-five years old. All our assets were seized.

The newspapers talked about misappropriation of funds. In Morocco, it's a crime to take money out of the country.

We can see Gibraltar from the plane. I fall asleep. The pressure drops suddenly. It wakes me up. I can see Nice in the distance. The plane lands. I already feel better.

As soon as we're off the plane, I hurry to the toilets to take out the cheque that's tucked under my knicker elastic. It was really irritating me. I feel free at last. I think we're finally out of danger.

Le Mirage

Victor, I call out your name so you might hear it.
So that my voice might reach you across the Atlantic.
I couldn't get back to sleep.
It's morning.
I can feel that slimy thing in my belly again.
I don't know why I agreed to take the pills.
I'm on the shore of Sidi Abderrahmane.
Dawn is plunging the coast into a chill, polarising fog.

I'm sweating. The tide is high. Sidi Abderrahmane is cut off.
I asked reception to call me a taxi.
The taxi drops me off in front of Mira Ventos.
My home is derelict. As though it's dead. But I know its story. I know how beautiful it has been. I know all the life it sheltered.
I'd like to shake off the years. Go back into the past. Listen to the sound of the water. Smell the plants again.
Mira Ventos is withered and abandoned. I want to cry but I can't.
I push open the gate, with all its silvery scales of peeling paint.
I lie down in the garden.
The ground is as hard as rock.

Soon it is evening. I must leave Mira Ventos and go back to the hotel before it's dark.

As I leave, I turn around to take one last look at my home.

It isn't called Mira Ventos any more.
It's called Le Mirage.
I hadn't noticed.

Sidi Abderrahmane

It's the end of the day.

When the sun is low in the west and the evening call to prayer sounds out through the streets of Casablanca and its echoes are lost to the sea.
Sidi Abderrahmane is shrouded in mist.
When the wind clears a space in the cloud, you can see the white limestone fortress washed by the sea.
The beach is huge.
The causeway of rocks polished by the waves leads to the sanctuary.

Allahu Akbar, you hear in the distance.

She feels alone. Disillusioned.
VICTOR
VICTOR

Her voice rings out in echoes that intermingle with those of the evening call to prayer.
ALLAHU AKBAR

Sidi Abderrahmane.
She is confronted with herself.
She doesn't want to live any more.

She wants to join all the women who've been going to Sidi Abderrahmane since the dawn of time.
All those desperate women. All those women who couldn't have children. Who couldn't go on living that way.
It is as though she is irresistibly drawn to the island sanctuary.
The tide is starting to come in.
She steps across the water that will soon cover the rocks.
I am no longer myself. I am her. I am the clown of Casablanca. I am all those women who have gone to the island fortress.
I'm walking towards Sidi Abderrahmane.
I too want to forget.
Forget everything.
I'm almost there.
But what can I hear?
Weeping.
These women do not want to die.
I can hear them crying out for life.

These women are prisoners of the stone forever.
I see them struggling. They cannot get away. They are dead.
In the distance the imams are waiting.
They are waiting for me.
Few women have ever come back from there.
Nobody really knows what goes on there.
The ones who have escaped have come home mad, and sometimes pregnant.
It is the last resort for women who can't have children.
The imams are waiting.
I close my eyes.
The imams are raping the women.
I can hear them crying out for life.
I no longer want to die.

I no longer want to go to Sidi Abderrahmane.
I want to turn back.
I can't any more.
The tide has already covered half of the path.
A huge wave crashes into me.
I am carried away by the sea.

Lemons as big as grapefruit.
The taste of mint tea.
My grandfather's warm embrace.
My cousins laughing in the moonlight. The zellige-tiled fountain and its water softly singing.
Light filtering through half-open shutters.
The warm body of the beloved.
The feeling of sunshine on skin.
Getting my head above the water.
Above the icy water that's carrying me away forever.
Tahiti Beach.
The taste of pistachio.
Alexandre's blond curls.
The reverie of the first kiss.
My grandfather holding my hand.
Above the water.
Hold your head above the water.
Hold on.

I have a terrible headache.
I wake up.
I have just escaped death.
It's morning.
The shore is unbelievably bright.

After we got back to France, Mum's belly got bigger. She was expecting my sister.

When my sister was born, she had a lump on her head just where Grandpa had been hit with the bust of Juba.

In the hotel lobby I talked about the clown of Casablanca. I hadn't seen her since I got back. It was as if she'd disappeared from the shore of Sidi Abderrahmane.
Somebody told me a big black Mercedes had come to fetch her.
Somebody told me the man who had once abandoned her was in the car.

The voice:

'Do you really think you loved him?'

Her:

'I don't know. I loved his face. It told a story.'

The voice:

'Was it a good story?'

Her:

'No.'

The White Wall

I've hired a convertible and decided to do a trip around the country before going back to Paris.
I'm no longer afraid of Victor, of life, of myself.
I'm filled with a need to live life, not intensely but to the full.

My fingers grip the Bakelite of the steering wheel, something tangible that helps me to cope with this new freedom echoing with loneliness. Before heading out of Casablanca, I drive past Mira Ventos. I automatically follow the route I used to take with Grandpa. The big villas, tended by caretakers, with their beautiful, lush gardens, line the road. I go beyond the white wall where Grandpa used to make me turn around.
A few metres further on, the beautiful, wide, tarred avenue becomes a narrow, unsurfaced track.
The tyres cautiously bump along in the gravel.
The track leads to a neighbourhood that looks like a shantytown.
Children dressed in rags come running towards me.
They hang onto the car. I accelerate, my heart in my mouth. I do a U-turn.
The narrow, sandy track. The villas barricaded behind brightly coloured hedges. The caretakers standing outside their respective properties, exchanging knowing looks.
I understand why Grandpa didn't want to go beyond the white wall.
I understand that the sunny world of my childhood wasn't Morocco, it was Mira Ventos.

I had never suffered before my grandfather was murdered.
Mira Ventos – an enchanted place cut off from the rest of the world.
I think about my grandfather's murderers, who believed the bust of Juba II was a bust of Christ.
They lived in poverty, with opulence in their faces.
The life we lived at Mira Ventos seems obscene to me.
The sumptuous parties.
The festival of Eid al-Adha, the men full of joy, giving praise.
The warm smell of méchoui, the traditional slow-roasted lamb, wafting out into the narrow, sandy track and drifting through the shantytown, where mothers are listening to their children crying of hunger.
I think about Victor, his beauty – a marble statue falling upon my body of glass.
Toothless children hanging onto the Bakelite steering wheel.
Mira Ventos, which is no longer Morocco.
Mira Ventos, a world apart.
Mira Ventos and a tragedy waiting to happen.
And us – bathed in sunlight on long summer afternoons, with the fountain softly singing.
I think of Nan Goldin's photograph.
Look beyond the surface.
Look beyond Victor's appearance.
Beyond intuition.
Look beyond experience.
I think the man in the photo looks kind. Yes, why not the pleasure of tobacco after the pleasure of the body? He puts down his cigarette and turns towards the woman lying on the bed. He kisses her. Nan smiles.
I think of Eduardo Mallea's words: 'Each man's destiny is personal only insofar as it may resemble what is already in his memory.'
I do another U-turn. I don't want my destiny to lie in my memories. I don't want to be a prisoner of my past.
I drive along the narrow, sandy track.

Moving towards the unexpected. Seeing and hearing what we cannot plan out.
A boy asks me where I'm going.
He speaks good French.
I say, 'I don't know.'
In a voice full of life and light-heartedness, he asks me, 'Will you take me home?'
'Where do you live?'
'Taroudant.'
I nod.
He gets in the car.
I wanted an extraordinary, incredible, life-saving, self-confirming adventure.

The hospitality offered by this boy and his family in the mountains.
A climb up to a dam. Golden sunlight.
Palm trees full of dates.
Couscous quite different from any I had had before.
Immersion in a Morocco I didn't know.
They introduce me to a French guy who wants to open an eco-hotel.
They tell me he's someone. That he rubs shoulders with important people in France.
I talk to him.
He's a man with vision who is drawn to Morocco.
At the top of the dam.
In bright sunshine.
Looking across at the mountain, with its red earth.
I close my eyes.
I'm looking for Mira Ventos, Le Mirage Hotel, Tahiti Beach.

I no longer have a home.
Home is with my grandmother, my mother, my grandfather.

Grandma has lost her mind. Mum plunged into chronic depression after the tragedy. Grandpa is dead and buried.
You can't 'lose the quotidian south'*, you can't lose your bearings when you no longer have any bearings to lose.
Before you can escape, you have to be a prisoner.
Make yourself a prisoner of your memories.
I decide to leave.

Mira Ventos.
The images pile one on top of another.
Huge playground of my childhood.
Lunches out in the sun.
Equestrian displays on moonlit summer evenings.
Mirrors covered with white sheets.
Torn Persian carpets.
My grandfather's blood at the foot of the white marble staircase.
Hassan looking at me with hatred.
The bougainvillea.
The room stinking of conspiracy.
The white wall.
What lies behind it.

---

*Quotation from 'Perdre le Midi quotidien' by Victor Segalen

Nan

1984. Nan does a self-portrait a month after being beaten by Brian. She nearly lost her left eye as a result of her injuries.

Mira Ventos

Before returning the car, I want to see Mira Ventos one last time.
Just to imprint it on my mind forever.
There's a builder's board. It looks as though it's been sold.
Twenty-one days travelling around and the cranes have already moved into the sorry garden.

I don't know what to think.
A hand on my shoulder.
I turn.
It's Alexandre.
He is just as I would have imagined him.
He has the same look in his eye.
He smiles at me.
I smile back.
Alexandre asks me, 'What do you want to call it?'
I tell him, 'Mira Ventos.'

At Le Mirage Hotel

Years before.
A deflated balloon has washed up on the beach.
Inside it, there's a piece of paper folded in four.
I undo the string.
I blow up the balloon and burst it.
I unfold the paper.
There's nothing written on it.

I've always kept that piece of paper. It's the only thing I've kept from Morocco.

Before driving off in the old convertible, I took out the piece of paper, yellowed with age.

I wrote two words on it in black felt tip:

Mira Ventos
Facing the Wind

La Blanche

I wake up. I'm sweating. It's almost morning. The early light is filtering through the horizontal slats of the shutters, which are closed tight. I look for him. Next to me. Alexandre isn't there. He's gone. Him too. Did he even exist?

I'm not sure.

I know I no longer had the strength to hold onto Alexandre or the image of Alexandre.

Alexandre-Victor.

Their faces merge. Commingle. Elude reality. My reality.

To forget. To forget oneself.

I prefer to look at the ceiling.

A fixed point so as not to founder. But my eye loses the fixed point. Gets lost.

Facing the void.

Scream. No. I don't want to.

I see myself again, smashing the door in.

I prefer silence.

Walling myself up in silence. Waiting.

I get out of bed.

I take the white sheets. I drape them over the mirror.

I put on a white cotton kaftan.

The one Mum wore for mourning.

I look in Grandma's drawers. There's lots of make-up, reds, white, black.

Plunging forlorn fingers into the colourful textures.
Reassuring materiality. Soothing.
Fingers covered with gouache, stroking my face.
Smiling at the other woman. The one who has suffered.
Yes, bury her beneath thick layers.
So you can no longer recognise her.
Leaving her childhood dreams behind her.
Her grandfather dead and buried.
Her child beneath the water.
Victor.
Alexandre's mocking laugh.
'Confuse all.' Change everything about.
Become Nothingness again.
Yes, disappear behind a mask that would no longer be her.

Sidi Abderrahmane.
Gritty sand.
She is pacing the shore of Sidi Abderrahmane.
Bare feet. A little girl and her mother in the distance.
The little girl is looking at her.
The wind carries their voices to her.
Sibilant. Haunting. Unreal.
The little girl to her mother:
'Look, Mummy. She scares me. I want to go.'
The mother:
'It's the clown of Casablanca. She's been pacing the shore of Sidi Abderrahmane forever.'
The little girl stares at her.
Look away.
No.
Their eyes meet. Hold. They hold each other's gaze.
A straight line is drawn between their lives.

She is waiting for the little girl to show her disgust. She's afraid.
The little girl smiles.
She steps forward.
Her mother takes her hand. Holds it. Holds her back.
The little girl and her mother walk away and disappear.
The only sound is the wind blowing across the huge beach.
It is misty.
I decide to go home.
Night is falling.

It is Dark

It is dark.
It is late.
A loud noise.
My grandparents' bedroom door is double-locked.
Grandma is asleep.
My grandfather tries to find where my grandmother has put the key.
He finds it in the drawer of the bedside table.
The key is in the door.
It is dark.
It is late.
In my sleep, I cry out to my grandfather:
'Don't turn the key.'
He turns it.
The door opens.

On 18 February 2002, Albert Pilot (aged 80) and Geneviève Pilot (78) are found lying dead in a pool of blood.
Their son, Henri Pilot, is found guilty of double murder.
Les Champs Élysées sous la pluie *is in a storage unit in Poitiers.*
Uncle has left Morocco.
Nobody knows what's become of him.
Fatima is leading a quiet life, living with her policeman brother.
Victor is doing travel programmes on television.
Mum has never got over her father's death and is living cloistered away in a two-room apartment in the south of France.
Grandma is still writing letters to the King of Morocco to get the case re-opened.
We still don't know who commissioned the crime against my grandfather.
Grandma has written one last book: Lettre à l'invisible.

Acknowledgements

I'd like to thank the whole team at Parthian, especially Richard Davies, Alison Evans and Carly Holmes, for their kindness, dedication and expertise in enabling me to bring *La Blanche* to an English-speaking readership. It's been a real pleasure to work with you all. Special thanks also to my friend, colleague and first reader, Anne-Marie Bizart, for her wise suggestions, gentle corrections and some sparkling discussions of all manner of things. This translation would be the poorer without you. And my love and thanks to Toby and Cal, Mandy and Kate, and a wonderful community of friends, writers and translators, near and far.

PARTHIAN

CARNIVALE

2019/21

La Blanche

Maï-Do Hamisultane

Translated by Suzy Ceulan Hughes

ISBN 978-1-91-268123-5

£8.99 • Paperback

The Night Circus and Other Stories

Uršuľa Kovalyk

Translated by Julia and Peter Sherwood

ISBN 978-1-91-268104-4

£8.99 • Paperback

Fiction in Translation

The Book of Katerina

Auguste Corteau

Translated by Claire Papamichael

ISBN 978-1-91-268126-6

£8.99 • Paperback

A Glass Eye

Miren Agur Meabe

Translated by Amaia Gabantxo

ISBN 978-1-91-210954-8

£8.99 • Paperback

Her Mother's Hands

Karmele Jaio

Translated by Kristin Addis

ISBN 978-1-91-210955-5

£8.99 • Paperback